Southern Ill. State Normal University

The Sphinx

Vol. 1

Southern Ill. State Normal University

The Sphinx
Vol. 1

ISBN/EAN: 9783337389864

Printed in Europe, USA, Canada, Australia, Japan

Cover: Foto ©Andreas Hilbeck / pixelio.de

More available books at **www.hansebooks.com**

Volume I.

Donohue, Henneberry & Co.,

PRINTERS, PUBLISHERS AND BINDERS,

CHICAGO.

1898   1899

A stupendous compilation of facts,
fiction, history and lies.

——————

THE SPHINX.

HURRAH FOR US.

——————

By the Class of 1900.

——————

SOUTHERN ILLINOIS NORMAL UNIVERSITY,
CARBONDALE, ILL.

Editor-in-Chief.

PHYSICAL TRAINING CLASS, S. I. N. U.—FIRST HOUR.

D. B. Parkinson.

TO

DANIEL BALDWIN PARKINSON, Ph. D.

OUR HONORED PRESIDENT, LOVED
AND INSPIRING TEACHER, THIS
RECORD OF THE SAYINGS
AND DOINGS OF THE
S. I. S. N. U.

Is respectfully dedicated.

The Board of Editors.

GREETING.

HISTORY records the fact that Egypt has given to the world many useful products. During the century just closing another Egypt has appeared in the arena of action. Not the Oriental country through which the Nile flows, but the garden spot of the great " Prairie State," Southern Illinois.

The Junior class of newer Egypt's leading educational institution sends forth this Annual, a record of the acts and sayings of the Normal University people.

The class, knowing that the readers of this book are fond of wrestling with abstruse problems, has christened it the Sphinx.

The Editorial Board has striven earnestly to give a true picture of student life as it exists to-day.

It has labored under many disadvantages, and whatever success it has achieved is largely due to the hearty co-operation and efficient aid of the classes and faculty.

We trust the Alumni will feel that the Annual reflects credit upon their Alma Mater.

EDITORIAL BOARD.

J. Oscar Marberry, Editor-in-Chief.
Roy F. B. Davis, Business Manager.

A. J. Reef, Artist.
F. B. F. Smith, Poet.

Bertha Spence.
I. Victor Iles.
Thos. J. Layman.
Simeon Boomer.
Nora Stewart.
Hattie H. Bowyer.

DANIEL BALDWIN PARKINSON, PH. D.

FOR a quarter of a century the State of Illinois has maintained at Carbondale an institution for the preparation of teachers. At the head of
this Normal have been strong educators, each of whom has added to
the success of his predecessor. Daniel Baldwin Parkinson, our honored
President, is the fourth president of this institution.

He was born in Highland, Madison County, Illinois, on the 6th of
September, 1845, and prepared himself for college in the schools of that
county. He entered McKendree College, September, 1864, and after four
years of earnest collegiate work graduated in the Scientific course, receiving the degree of Bachelor of Science.

For one year he was superintendent of the schools at Carmi, White
Co., Ill. For three years he filled the Chair of Natural Sciences in Jen-
nings Seminary, at Aurora, Kane County, Ill.

In 1873 he entered Northwestern University, at Evanston, and for one
year did post-graduate work in that institution.

When the first Board of Trustees of the Southern Normal came to fill
the Chair of Physics and Chemistry, they selected this very successful student and teacher for this responsible position; hence Dr. Parkinson has
been connected with this institution ever since its founding. In 1874 he
received the degree of Master of Arts from McKendree College.

He was made registrar and vice-president in 1892; August, 1897, the
Board appointed him acting president, to fill the vacancy left by the resignation of Dr. Everest. Shortly afterwards, McKendree College conferred
upon him the degree of Doctor of Philosophy.

March, 1898, the Board of Trustees elected him president, and the
faculty and students organized a surprise party in his honor.

PHYSICAL TRAINING SCHOOL, S. L. N. U. SECOND HOUR.

MISS MARTHA BUCK, who holds the chair of English Grammar at the S. I. N. U., was educated at Chicago, and Aurora. She was nine years in public school work in the State of Illinois, and in 1874 came to the position which she has since held in this institution. Miss Buck has long been an authority in grammar, and has embodied her ideas on that difficult subject in a series of grammars, published in 1895.

MISS MARTHA BUCK.

GEORGE H. FRENCH was educated at the Cortlandville Normal School in New York. Taught four years in the country schools of that State. Later he was superintendent of schools at South Belvidere, and Roscoe, Illinois, and Grand Rapids, Wisconsin. For nine years, professor of sciences in College of Agriculture, coming to Carbondale as Assistant State Entomologist in 1877. In the following year he was elected to the position which he now holds in this institution. On science, especially, Prof. French is authority in both America and Europe.

GEORGE HAZEN FRENCH, M.A.

MATILDA F. SALTER

MISS MATILDA F. SALTER, teacher of Art and Drawing at the Southern Illinois Normal University, was educated at the Bettie Stuart Institute, Springfield, Illinois, and Cooper Institute of Art, New York. She was one year assistant principal of schools at Chester, Illinois, and in the year 1885 was elected to the position which she now holds with credit to herself and with honor to the institution.

GEORGE W. SMITH, M.A.

GEORGE W. SMITH, M. A. (Blackburn University, 1893), began his teaching as a country teacher in Greene county, Illinois. Five years were spent in this work. Two years as principal of the White Hall, Ill., schools; one year as principal of the Perry, Pike county, Ill., schools; four years as superintendent of the White Hall schools; seven years as training teacher in this school. Two years ago the two departments of History and Geography were combined and Mr. Smith was selected as head of the department. He attended Blackburn University and the Cook County Normal.

SAMUEL B. WHITTINGTON was educated at Ewing College and at Danvile, Ind. He was superintendent of the Benton, Ill., schools four years; three years at Ava, Ill., and two years at Mt. Vernon, Ill. In 1893 he came to this school as assistant in Mathematics. In 1897 he was transferred to the department of Physical Training, having completed a course in the Milwaukee Normal School for physical training.

SAMUEL B. WHITTINGTON.

SAMUEL E. HARWOOD, M. A.

SAMUEL E. HARWOOD, M. A. (Indiana University, 1892), has charge of the department of Mathematics. His career as a teacher began in a log school house three miles north of Carbondale. He was in the public school work in Indiana for eleven years, being superintendent of the Spencer and Atica schools. In 1893 he came to this school as head of the department of Mathematics. Prof. Harwood is an earnest student of educational theory and has contributed largely to educational journals, and is the author of "Notes on Method in Arithmetic," which is largely used as a text in method classes.

CARLOS EBEN ALLEN.

CARLOS EBEN ALLEN, Chair of Languages, graduated from the classic course at Carleton College, Northfield, Minn., in 1894. In 1893-4 he was tutor in Latin at the Northfield Academy. In the same year of his graduation at the Carleton College, he was elected to the chair of Languages S. I. N. U. This position he has since held with entire satisfaction.

HENRY W. SCHRYOCK is the faculty orator. He graduated in high school at Olney and received his degree of Ph. B. at Illinois Wesleyan. He taught for eleven years in the Olney High School and came to this institution in 1893, in chair of literature and elocution. Chemistry has since been added and elocution subtracted. One year was spent in Chicago University.

HENRY W. SCHRYOCK, Ph. B., Registrar

JAMES KIRK, A.M.

JAMES KIRK, A. M., prepared for college in Washington Seminary. Pursued the college course at Eureka College, and received the A. B. degree in June, 1871. Received the A. M. degree in 1874, taught in Eureka College from 1876 to 1884. Has taught in country school; has been superintendent of schools of Woodford county, and of Washburn, Minonk and Pekin, Illinois, and assistant to the State Superintendent of Public Instruction. Came to Carbondale in September, 1895.

JAMES H. BROWNLEE, M. A.

JAMES H. BROWNLEE, M. A., was born in 1846. He served in the civil war with a Kansas regiment. He graduated from McKendree College, Lebanon, Ill., in 1870, with the degree of A. B., and a few years later received from his *alma mater* an M. A. He held the chair of Elocution and Literature here for eleven years, filled the same Chair in University of Illinois for nine years, and was recalled here in 1897.

MISS WERTZ received her education at Bloomington, Ill., and at the University of Minnesota. She held responsible positions as teacher and supervisor in Bloomington for twelve years. She spent five years in Minneapolis as supervising principal and received her training there as a primary teacher under Sarah L. Arnold, now of Boston. In 1896 she entered the S. I. N. U. as student of pedagogy under Prof. Kirk, and in 1897 was returned as principal of primary school and training teacher of first six grades.

ADDA P. WERTZ.

ELIZABETH PARKS.

ELIZABETH PARKS, assistant training teacher, is an alumnus of the Normal University, a member of the class of 1889. After graduation she taught one year at Coulterville, four years at Du Quoin, and in 1897 was appointed to the position she now holds.

WASHINGTON B. DAVIS, A. M.

WASHINGTON BEATY DAVIS, A. M. graduated from Wabash College, Crawfordsville, Ind., 1880, in classical course Was principal at Friendsville two years superintendent at Fairfield six years superintendent at Nokomis three years. For five years he was principal of the Department of Preparatory School and professor of the chair of history at Blackburn University, Carlinsville Ilinois, and superintendent at Pittsfield two years. Came here in 1897. Principa of High School.

FRANK H. COLYER, A. B. Professor Colyer is an aluminus of this institution, class of 1889. He received his degree of A. B. from Indian University, and has attended Chicago University one year. He was superintendent at Brown's and Albion, Ill., and at Peola, Ind. He came to the chair of assistant in geography and history in the S. I. N. U. in 1897.

FRANK H. COLYER.

MARY M. McNEILL.

MARY M. McNEILL graduated from Almira College, at Greenville, Ill. She received her musical education from private tutors in St. Louis and at the College of Music in Cincinnati. After doing studio work as a teacher of music she was called to the chair of instrumental music at the Normal in 1897.

MINNIE J. FRYAR.

MISS MINNIE J. FRYAR (class of '86, S. I. N. U.) taught in Anna, Carbondale and Clinton, Iowa, six years in all. In 1892 she was elected librarian at her old alma mater, which position she has since held with credit, having indexed the library according to the modern Dewey system. She has also done other efficient work.

MISS AUGUSTA MCKINNEY was educated at the S. I. N. U. She taught eight years in the public schools of Carbondale, after which she worked with Meyer Brothers Drug Co., St. Louis, until she came here in the summer of 1897 as stenographer and clerical assistant.

AUGUSTA MCKINNEY.

HARRY J. ALVIS.

PHYSICAL TRAINING CLASS, S. I. N. C.—THIRD HOUR.

DR. ROBT. ALLYN.

DR. ROBERT ALLYN.

IN the arms of the protecting elms among the hills of old Connecticut, more than half a century ago, nestled a little white schoolhouse.

Within was the droning hum of whispered study and the scratch of pencils on the slate, as the little urchins worked their sums, while at the scant blackboard the classes ciphered, or, ranged around the wall, held a spelling match. There were praises for the boy who went head, but woe to the luckless chap who was turned down to the other end. The teacher of this school was a tall, spare youth of eighteen, disconcerted, possibly, at the giggles of the older girls, but very much in earnest, teaching his first school for the then magnificent sum of eleven dollars a month.

This youth was Robert Allyn, born at Ledyard, Connecticut, January 25, 1817. His father was an intelligent farmer, but could not send his son beyond the common schools. But the young man, then only a boy, was not to be baffled by circumstances. While working on the farm, without a teacher he commenced the study of Latin and Algebra.

As we have said, he taught his first school at the age of eighteen, and was so successful that he was in demand, and in a few years got his pocket-book in condition to attend school again. His secondary training came from the Wesleyan Academy, in Wilbraham, Mass. At the age of twenty, in 1837, he began his college course at Wesleyan University, at Middletown, Conn. It is no small praise to say that he stood at the head of his class, a class that was so full of eminent scholars, the class of '41.

His specialty was mathemetics, and immediately upon his graduation he was called to the chair of mathemetics in the Wesleyan Academy. But as teachers filled more than one chair at a time then, we may see him again in the class room, no longer a youth, teaching this time Latin. And in that Virgil class are two men who will come to honor, even greater, perhaps, than their teacher. One is the late Oliver Marcy, always a teacher, and devoted for more than twenty-five years to the interests of Northwestern University, and always a scientist, noted especially in geological circles, and known demoninationally as the Methodist Agassiz. The other is Gilbert Haven, the Methodist Bishop. Prof. Allyn was honored with the presidency of the Academy at Wilbraham, and held the position several years.

But he was induced to take charge, as chancellor and president, of the Providence Conference Seminary, a denominational school which, under his management, worked its way up from obscurity to a place in the first rank among institutions doing preparatory work.

From this institution he was elected state Commissioner of Education for the state of Rhode Island. This office he resigned to accept the Chair of Ancient Languages in Ohio University. When the anti-slavery contest was on he did not hesitate to enter the field of politics. At the solicitation of his friends he "stumped" the state of Ohio, preaching abolition and temperance. He was twice elected to the legislature and did not fail to open his mouth against evil, as do some good men that get into legislatures. They are good—for nothing.

During the Civil War, for four years, he was president of the Wesleyan Female College of Cincinnati.

In '64 he made one more move west, to the presidency of McKendree College in Lebanon, Ill. During the ten years he served here many people we know graduated from that College. Prof. Brownlee and Dr. Parkinson are partly the work of this great man, as is Judge Harker of Carbondale, and countless others we do not know.

When in 1874 the first building of the Southern Illinois State Normal University at Carbondale was finished, the board of trustees could find no man with the necessary executive ability, coupled with such a rugged intellectuality, as Dr. Robert Allyn. He was made president of the infant institution, and from that time its history is his history, for during the rest of his life his whole energy was turned to making this institution, though one of the state, a factor for Christian Education.

In his work he was ever faithful, ever at his post. When the first building burned, he, with the assistance of the rest of the faculty, set the students to work at taking out the library, desks and costly apparatus. Then he disappeared from the crowd. As the flames kept creeping on toward the north end of the building, Prof. Inglis became alarmed and dashed up to the president's office, on the top floor, which was the fourth in that building. Bursting into the room Prof. Inglis saw the Doctor calmly making valuable papers into bundles, sorting them out of a desk too heavy to move. The Professor shouted to the Doctor to come out of the building; his life was too precious to be lost. The Doctor looked at the upper corner of the room, from which smoke was rolling, and said, "Not yet, Professor; I am not quite through." The Professor urged him again, and another member of the faculty came to bring him down, but the Doctor told them he would get through quicker if they did not talk so much. Under this they were silent, and about five minutes later, with all the papers, they got the Doctor out of the room, while the tiny flames were already playing and darting along the walls and ceiling.

During the interim between the fire and the new building, Dr. Allyn kept the school running and graduated the usual classes each year. In the new building he served five years. Twice, having passed the limit of three score years and ten, he tendered his resignation; but not until 1892, having served as president eighteen years, and arrived at the age of seventy-five, could he persuade the board of trustees to accept it.

For two years more he lived to bless, to encourage, to inspire, and, on a Sunday morning, just as the joyous church bells were ringing their welcome call, his spirit passed away.

Dear is his memory to his few living classmates; dear to the students of his loved *alma mater*, among whose many noble sons he ranks not the lowest; dear to those institutions in which he first taught and presided; dearer to those who learned at his desk, both in school and in college; dearer to those who have worked with him to uplift, instruct and inspire the young, and dearest to that institution which is his monument and his alone.

In the parlor of this Normal there hangs a portrait of heroic size of this heroic man. His name is one more added to the long list of this country, and of New England, of men who have risen by their own efforts, and by ability to positions of honor, of opportunity. He was an educator with common sense. He was an executor of noble generosity. He was a Christian with ambition. Look at that portrait; study those features; be inspired by him and thou shalt be like him.

ALUMNI.

ARTHUR ROBERTS.
Class of 1897.

A. L. BLISS.
Class of 1892.

O. A. HARKER, JR.
Class of 1896.

JOHN P. GILBERT.
Class of 1896.

W. C. FLY.
Class of 1898.

A. EUGENE WILLIAMS.
Class of 1894.

EDWARD LONGBONS.
Class of 1894.

J. O. KARRAKER.
Class of 1896.

W. T. MARBERRY.
Class of 1897.

SENIOR CLASS.

STEWART. BÖMLE. CRAWFORD. HALDAMAN. McKITRICK. BRAINARD. McCONAGHIE. BLAKE.
CONE. MURPHEY. GROVE. BREWSTER. ROE. PALMER. BRAINARD.

SENIOR CLASS.

COLORS—Green and White.

OFFICERS.

Orville Marion Karraker, President.
Myrtle Irene Palmer, Vice-President.
Edith Authea Roe, Secretary.
Willis Gerard Cisne, Treasurer.
John Woods Marchildon, Sergeant-at-Arms.

CLASS ROLL.

English-Latin Course.

Libbie Marie Brewster,   Orville Marion Karraker,
Besse Lillian Grove,   John Woods Marchildon,
Josephine Stewart.

English Course.

J. M. Etherton,   F. C. Pruett,
F. D. McKittrick,   Stuart Brainard,
Margaret Haldaman,   Carl Webekemeyer,
Myrtle I. Palmer,   Pearl Brainard,
W. G. Cisne,   Edith A. Roe,
W. O. Harris,   W. G. Murphey,
Ida Kell,   Thomas McConaghie,
Lizzie Elder,   Hester M. Duncan,
J. E. Crawford,   J. P. Cowan,
Lula D. Hooker,   E. L. Blake.

YE SENIORS, '99.

GIRLS.

EDITH A. ROE, Carbondale.

Attended Carbondale High School two years and S. I. N. U. as special
student two terms. Regular Normal course four years. Completes
English course with two years Latin extra. Employed to teach school
near Campbell Hill next winter term.

MRS. LULA DAVIS HOOKER, Carbondale.

Attended High School and taught three years in Tennessee. Has been
student at S. I. N. U. nine terms. Expects to teach in Dresden High
School, Tennessee. Graduates from English course.

JOSEPHINE STEWART, Carbondale.
> Student in S. I. N. U. fourteen terms. Graduates from English-Latin course. Has taught two terms.

MARGARET HALDAMAN, Decatur.
> Graduates from English course, but took one year each of Latin and German. Has taught five years. Spent thirteen terms in S. I. N. U.

A. PEARL BRAINARD, Carbondale.
> Graduated from Carbondale High School. Attended S. I. N. U. four years. Graduates from English course.

MYRTLE IRENE PALMER.
> Graduates from the English course. Two years Latin. Attended S. I. N. U. four years.

BESSIE LILLIAN GROVE, Carbondale.
> Graduated from Carbondale High School. Six years student in S. I. N. U. Two years special work. Four years Normal.

LIBBIE MARIE BREWSTER, Carbondale.
> Eight years in school at S. I. N. U. Two in High School. Graduates from English-Latin course. Took special work in German, Trigonometry and Analytical Geometry.

THE SENIOR BOYS.

SINCE gray hairs demand respect, we commence with the aged and proceed toward the more modern. First comes the Potato King of Southern Illinois, JAMES ETHERTON, whose entire attendance at the S. I. N. U. covers a period of over seventeen years. He is married and has acquired quite a fortune; he talks no Latin.

F. D. McKITTRICK, next in chronological endowments, is also a married man. He is quite noted as a High School principal, but better known as the Baby Elephant, as his avoirdupois defeats the scales at 218. He finishes in the English course with two years of Latin.

J. E. CRAWFORD, who has less between him and the sunlight than most men, finishes in the English course and performs more gracefully in the gymnasium than any body, excepting McKITTRICK.

W. O. HARRIS, a graduate of Southern Illinois College at Enfield, is a good student, especially in Philosophy, and even dares to try bluffs on Prof. Kirk. English course.

Rev. Dr. Chas. Webekemeyer, popularly known as the "Grand Old Man," although he has had plenty of Latin and knows more "dutch" than the Emperor of Germany, will receive his sheepskin for only the English course.

Edward Blake, executive in the Socratic society, has no degree but gets there just the same. He is great in debate, a logical thinker.

Thos. McConaghie hangs out the sign for the rest of the Seniors, "Position Wanted." He formerly attended Sparta High School; is an athlete; a short course man.

Willis Gerard Cisne is the brilliant man whose specialty is everything. He is a professional teacher and goes next year to Fairfield. He is a near relative to Prof. Buck, though like most Seniors only a short course man.

Stuart Brainard believes this creed: Ladies must be worshipped. He has a sister in the class, and if you know her you do not wonder at the creed. His specialty is Mathematics.

John Woods Marchildon weighs 68 lbs. 11 oz., but wears a bonnet fit for Jupiter Olympus. He is known in cultured circles as Marchildon of Thebes. He takes Trigonometry, Latin and German. He wants but little here below—A WIFE.

O. M. Karraker is class Czar. He knows what Marchildon does, and talks about the organism and spiritual essence.

W. G. Murphey has come up through the grades, and is one of the few who do so and graduate with honor. There is a place for him commencement week.

Chas. F. Pruett, last but not least in weight, is something of an athlete, captain of the football team, 1898. He is a High School graduate and can talk some Latin.

We recommend all of the above who are not married as good husbands.

CLASS SONG.

Words and music by G. B. Fields.

Dedicated to Senior Class of '99 of S. I. N. U.

Oh, the years have gone in their beauty,
    And the bright golden days have all fled;
While each hour filled with pleasure and duty,
    Is now numbered along with the dead.
Yet those moments now gone were not wasted—
    Tho' so quickly and pleasantly past,
For the pleasure of knowledge tasted,
    And sweet friendships were formed that will last.

CHORUS.

Farewell, oh, class of ninety-nine,
    May joy and peace be ever thine;
May friendship's chain each heart entwine,
    And make each life divine.

Oh, these book—haunted halls so familiar
    With each face full of friendship and cheer;
Linked in mind with each honest endeavor,
    To fond memory will often appear.
" By and by " when the years have flown o'er us
        And have crowned us with honor and love,
May the kind Heavenly Father permit us
        To be classmates and graduates above.

ODE TO THE SENIORS.

How dear to our hearts is the class of ninety-nine,
    When tender remembrances call them to view,
Their beauty, their excellence which ne'er can decline,
    And every good trait that man ever knew:
The wide-spreading earth in its glory and thrift,
    Beareth much fruit of merit and worth,
But broader than all are these Seniors so swift,
    As, poised on their dignity, they refrain from all mirth.
The dignified Seniors, the wide-spreading Seniors,
The pure-hearted Seniors of the class of ninety-nine.

These Seniors we know are true hearted and brave:
  Ready in their zeal to do good everywhere,
With song and with word they transform the knave,
  The "Prep." and the Freshman so tender and fair.
To me 'tis a source of deep, true-hearted pleasure
  To witness the work of these people I praise,
As they go about seeking in disconsolate measure,
  Those they may help to see better days.
The grand old Seniors, the bright-eyed Seniors,
The up-and-doing Seniors of the class of ninety-nine.

'Tis sweet to recall in the rush and commotion,
  Of the world's busy hum of commerce and trades;
That in thy ranks with a patriot's devotion,
  Stand stanch and true thy beautiful maids.
An honor to all are those girls with their lips
  So rosy and red with their truth overflowing;
For often at noon when at lunch the class sips,
  I have watched and longed with a hope that's still growing.
The rosy-cheeked Seniors, the red-lipped Seniors,
The long coveted Seniors of the class of ninety-nine.

I fancy to-day, as I look on the future,
  With all its promises of power and of health,
That not far distant it seemeth to you sure
  Your life will be happy, speaking greatness and wealth.
Blest be thy future, O, class of ninety-nine,
  Long may thy power rule the land and the sea,
To teach to thy sons as I shall teach mine,
  To come to the Normal and do as did we.
The God-favored Seniors, the loving, happy Seniors,
The old reliable Seniors of the class of ninety-nine.

So here's to your greatness, its usefulness and joy,
With Algebra and Pedagogy your minds to employ;
And if a consort your members wish to find,
Let them select from the Juniors of ninety-nine.
With humble Juniors to enhance your fame,
You will surely find an increased great name.
As a parting line, then, to thy power and pride,
May Heaven be thy refuge and the Lord be thy guide.
The intellectual Seniors, the purely moral Seniors,
The best of all the Seniors, the class of ninety-nine.

SENIOR CLASS STATISTICS.

NAME.	AGE.	WEIGHT.	HEIGHT.	FAVORITE SONG.
O. M. Karraker....	34	208	4-6	If You Love Me, Mr. H., Give Me '69.
J. M. Etherton.....	17	115	6-4	I Long to be an Artist.
F. D. McKittrick ..	3	93	4-9	I Am Monarch of All I Survey
Besse L. Grove.....	40	306	6-2	Because I Love You.
Libbie M. Brewster	25	96	5-8	I Was Dreaming.
J. W. Marchildon..	33⅓	204	6-3	Flower in the Crannied Wall.
Margie Haldaman..	16	89	5-9	Twinkle, Twinkle, Little Star.
Myrtle I. Palmer...	38	165	5-11¾	O, Happy Days Gone By.
W. G. Cisne	18	102	4-8	In the Gloaming, O My Darling
W. O. Harris......	23	125	6-½	And Pedagogy I Do Love.
Ida N. Kell........	9	88	4-6	Oh, Shall I Pass in Algebra?
Josie Y. Stewart...	5	45	4-3	O, How I Hate to Leave Thee.
F. C. Pruett......	13	200	5-10	Hail, The Conquering Hero Comes.
Stuart Z. Brainard.	36¾	148	5-9	Old Hundred.
C. A. Webekemeyer	16	170	4-11	Ninety-and-Nine.
Pearl B. Brainard..	21	109	5-8	Carry Me Back to Old Virginia
Edith C. Roe......	24⅓	109½	5-8¼	We Rock Away.
W. G. Murphy.....	31	157	6-0	I Would I Were a Senator.
T. D. McConaghie.	14	209	5-11	I Wish I Had a Mustache.
Lizzie E. Elder ...	17	97	5-10	America.
Hester M. Duncan.	18	123	5-11½	Steal Away.
J. E. Crawford	8	74	4-6	Get Thee a Wife.
J. P. Cowan.......	9	84	4-8	Get Thee a Wife.
Lulu D. Hooker....	19	90	6-0	Coronation.
E. L. Blake	15	149 9/10	6-1	After the Ball.
Total..........	493 5/12	3.376⅖	137-8	O, Had I a Turnip.

Composite Senior.
Born. June 15 - 1406 A.D.
Hright. 138 ft 8 in.
Wright. 1 ton 1376 lbs.

SENIOR ROASTS.

A Freshman hesitates on the word "connoisseur."
The Professor asked: "What would you call a man that pretends to know everything?"
Freshman answers: "A professor."

Freshman: "My Senior friend, have you a sufficient amount of confidence in a poor Freshman to lend him a dollar for a few days?"
Senior: "Oh, yes, I am sure I have the confidence, but I haven't got the dollar."

Mr. K. was once teaching a class in the training department when he had occasion to ask the following questions:
"Who in this class has ever seen an elephant's skin?"
"I have," shouted one.
"Where?" asked the anxious Mr. K.
"On the elephant," was the positive reply.

A Senior of the Class of '99 was being examined by a school board not long ago, and among the questions asked was the following:
A member of the Board: "Do you think the world is round or flat?"
Senior (as he scratched his head seemingly in deep thought): "Well, some people think one way and some another, and I'll teach round or flat, just as the parents please."

Professor: "Mr. W., you may tell me how many sides the mind has?"

Student: "Two sides, sir."

Professor: "What are they?"

Student: "An inside and an outside."

The professor was nonplused but continued: "I do not agree with you."

Student: "I do not wonder, Professor, for great minds differ sometimes.

Professor: "You compliment me unduly, sir."

Student: "Well pardon me, Professor, it was not my intention to so honor you."

The Professor would not be outdone so he asked; "Did you ever study cause and effect in the mind?"

Student: "Yes, sir."

Professor: "Does an effect ever go before a cause?"

"Student: Yes, sir.

"Professor: "Give me an instance?"

Student: "A man wheeling a barrow."

The class roared, and the Professor asked no more questions.

A SENIOR FISHING TALE.

When a noble Senior doth wish to angle,
A hook like this he loves to dangle:

His line it is both good and strong,
And he catches a fish about so long:

Before he gets home the fish doth grow,
And he tells his friends it measured so:

But the Juniors who have a fishing been,
Know that the Senior has fibbed like sin,
And they simply sit and smile and grin:

oho!   oho!   oho!   oho!

                                              ANONYMOUS.

A SENIOR PONY.

I.   A little Senior climbed his old man's knees,
Begged for a pony, " Do, papa, please!
Why can't I have one ?   Why work alone ?
Allen won't know it, I'll ride at home."

II.   " I had a pony years, years ago.
Where it is now, son, I'm sure I don't know.
I and my pony, I and my all,
Went from the Normal during the fall."

III.   After the long vacation,
After his grades are read,
After his father has sought him,
And wishes that he were dead;
Many a good intention,
If you but knew them all,
Are made on account of suspension,
During the fall.

IV.   I was quite happy, eased was my brain,
Thought how my wisdom would appear so very plain,
In recitation, O, but I was meek,
After my pony, I took a sneak.

V.   When I looked up, dear, there stood a man
Watching my pony as Allen can.
I and my pony, thrown in the hall,
Left the dear Normal during the fall.

SENIOR PONIES IN PASTURE

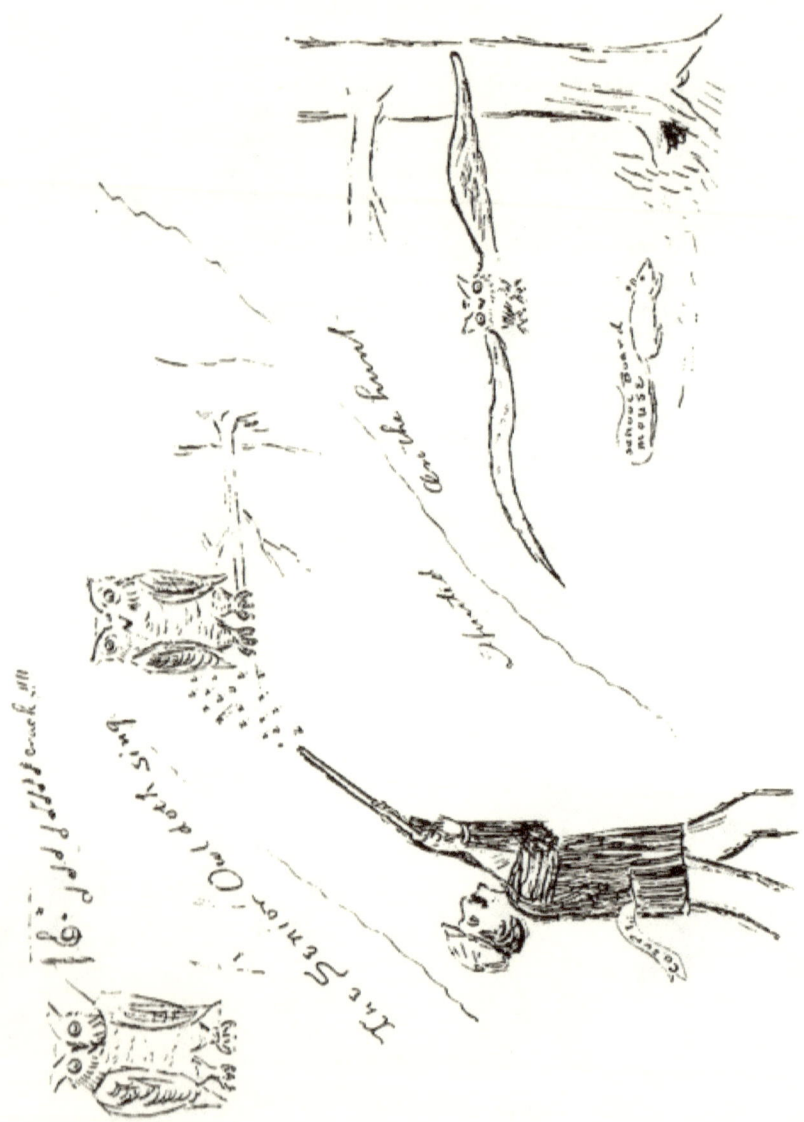

AN APPERCEPTIVE HALLUCINATION.

As the sun was slowly rising
  In the lovely month of May,
Tinging with its rosy brilliance
  Crests of hill-tops far away;
While drinking in the joys of nature
  I saw a youth of ninety-nine,
Who contemplated life with sadness,
  And for his distant home did pine.

"O, youth," said I, with heartfelt feelings
  Of pity, kindness, in my heart,
"How came you thus in grief to wander
  And from your happy friends to part?
Why wear you such a look of sorrow?"
  He gazed upon the rising sun
With gloom impressed upon his features,
  And thus his tale of woe begun.

"Once I was full of joy and gladness,
  Of gloomy thoughts I had no share;
Yet now I wear a look of sadness,
  To smile or laugh I do not dare.
As you wish to know the awful story
  Of my sad and cruel fate,
I'll strive with all my mental forces
  To tell it fresh and up to date.

"Once, in a class called Pedagogy,
  Where man and maiden, lad and lass,
Devote their souls to Rosenzkranz
  For fear that they will never pass;
Where Hegel, Herbart, mighty minds,
  Consort with Pestalozzi great;
Where one would never, never wish
  To fail and flunk, or hesitate.

"There, in solemn concourse gathered,
   Were many men of many minds.
'Mediocres' were well represented,
   Of 'block-heads' there were many kinds.
The 'Genius' (there was only one,
   As I am very pained to say)
Sat in the great professor's chair,
   Firing questions at me all that day.

"I answered some, I guessed at others,
   But gradually I lost my wit,
And stumbling rather worse than usual,
   In thunder tones he bade me 'SIT!'

           ✧   ✧

"I cared not much for empty honors,
   I only wished a grade.   Alas!
For since I made that noted failure
   My comrades whisper, 'He won't pass!'"

MAIN BUILDING.

HISTORY OF THE SOUTHERN ILLINOIS STATE NORMAL UNIVERSITY.

SOON after the close of the civil war, the leading spirits in the educational ranks of Southern Illinois recognized the fact that their end of the state was not receiving its share of state aid in the preparation of her teachers for the duties of the school-room. In the course of a few years this demand for a special training of teachers took definite shape in an act of the General Assembly of 1869, which was approved on April 20th, proivding for the erection and equipment of the Southern Illinois State Normal University. In compliance with said act, the Governor appointed the following named gentlemen to serve as trustees: Capt. Daniel Hurd of Cario; Gen. Eli Boyer of Olney; Col. Thomas M. Harris of Shelbyville; Rev. Elihu J. Palmer of Belleville; and Samuel Flanagan, Esq., of Benton.

The Board of Trustees adopted the usual but ofttimes unfortunate method of securing the location of the proposed institution by letting the matter of the selection of the site to the highest bidder. After the usual hot contest for such prizes, Carbondale was the chosen place, which was at that time the home of Gen. John A. Logan, who perhaps had more or less influence in securing this honor for the place of his residence and the county of his birth. This enterprising little village is located on the Illinois Central R. R., midway between Centralia and Cairo, fifty-six miles from the former and fifty-seven miles from the latter. The people of this place have ever been loyal to the school and the administration of its affairs.

The name of the school is quite pretentious. Possibly the explanation of the cause of so heavy a title, made by President Cook in his interesting account of the Illinois State Normal University, applies with equal propriety in this connection. It was the fond hope of some of the early friends of the school to have a much broader scope to the curriculum than that advocated by the more recent supporters of the Normal Schools. This plan, however, never took definite shape, and the institution soon settled down to its legitimate work, making the course as largely professional as possible under the circumstances. Its aim is to make it wholly so as soon as the conditions will allow it.

The contract for the building was given to Mr. James M. Campbell of Carbondale, for the sum of $225,000.00. Ground was broken, and on May 17, 1870, the corner-stone was laid with impressive ceremonies by Grand Master H. G. Reynolds, representing the Masonic fraternities of Illinois. This was an event that called together thousands of people to participate in an exercise that gave promise of a new era in educational interest. Such

SCIENCE BUILDING.

an occasion is full of meaning to a community that realizes its needs and appreciates the value of an educational institute in its midst. In the following spring the contractor was killed while superintending the erection of the building, and the work ceased till the next legislature appointed a Board of Building Commissioners, who took charge of the work and pushed it to a completion.

In September, 1873, Gov. John L. Beveridge appointed a new board, in compliance with the modified law affecting the case. This new board consisted of Hon. Thos. S. Ridgway of Shawneetown; Edwin S. Russell, Esq., of Mt. Carmel; Lewis M. Phillips, Esq., of Nashville; Judge Jacob W. Wilkins of Marshall; and Dr. James Roberts of Carbondale. Upon their organization, Oct. 28, 1873, Mr. Ridgway was made president and Dr. Roberts secretary. The total cost of the building is placed at $265,-000.00. It was dedicated with appropriate exercises on July 1, 1874. The principal address of the occassion was to have been delivered by Hon. Newton Bateman, then Superintendent of Public Instruction, but on account of sickness he was prevented from being present. His place was acceptably filled, however, by Dr. Richard Edwards, then President of the Illinois State Normal University. The other speakers for this notable occasion for Southern Illinois were Dr. Robert Allyn, who had been recently elected president of the institution; Dr. Charles H. Fowler, then President of the Northwestern University; Hon. J. J. Bird, of Cairo the President of the Board of Trustees.

The influence of Dr. Allyn, who served as president of the institution for eighteen years, and the able corps of teachers was decidedly for a high order of culture.

The first year closed with an enrollment of 396; with a constant increase in numbers and improved methods, together with enlarged facilities for work, the school grew in popular favor and usefulness.

On Nov. 26, 1883, this temple of learning was laid in ashes. By heroic efforts the furniture, library, and apparatus were saved from the flames. The citizens of Carbondale kindly provided for the work of the school to continue in churches, offices, etc., until their temporary home was completed. This one-story structure served as the home of the school until the completion of the present magnificient structure, Feb. 24, 1886. After an imposing dedication the faculty and students found themselves in one of the most commodious school buildings in the state.

The next event of special interest to the school was the resignation of Dr. Allyn, which took place publicly on commencement day, June 9, 1892. After eighteen years of faithful service at the head of the school, during

PRESIDENT'S OFFICE.

which time he had been a prominent member of State and National Educational Associations, he retired to the quiet of his home.

Dr. Allyn was succeeded by Prof. John Hull, a prominent professor of the institution.

A change in the state administration brought about a radical change in the administration of the Normal School, and Dr. H. W. Everest was placed at the head of the institution. The Doctor remained in charge four years, during which time the science building was constructed at a cost of $40,000. By his genial nature, kind disposition and scholarly attainments, Dr. Everest has won many friends throughout the state.

At present Dr. D. B. Parkinson is president of the institution. An interesting biography of our honored president will be found elsewhere.

During the twenty-five years of the school's existence, it has passed successfully through many trying scenes. And with its two grand buildings thoroughly equipped with the most modern apparatus, a library of nearly 15,000 volumes of good books, and guided by a very excellent faculty, who can tell the future of this school—the pride of Southern Illinois?

RECEPTION ROOM.

JUNIOR CLASS.

McANELLY.   DAVIS.   ILES.   SPANGLER.   PET.   LAYMAN.   MASHBERY.
PAYNE.   McGERAGHIL.   MERTZ.   BOWYER.   MARKON.

JUNIOR CLASS.

Motto: *Iubet vicissem.*   Colors: Crimson and Gold.

Yell: Hi, hi, hi, he, he, he,
M, D, C, C, C, C, Algebra, Pedagogy, Lightning, Thunder,
Century Class, Century Class, 1900.

Fact: We are the people.

OFFICERS:

T. B. F. Smith, President.
Tillie McConaghie, Vice-President.
May Fryar, Secretary.
J. I. McKnelly, Treasurer.
W. A. Brandon, Sergeant-at-Arms.

CLASS ROLL.

1. Boomer, Simeon
2. Bowyer, Hattie H.
3. Brandon, Wm. A.
4. Davis, Roy F. B.
5. Fryar, May
6. Iles, I. Victor
7. Layman, Thos. J.
8. Marron, Minnie
9. McConaghie, Tillie
10. McKnelly, Jacob I.
11. Mertz, Bertie B.
12. Marberry, J. Oscar
13. Reef, A. J.
14. Smith, T. B. F.
15. Spence, Bertha
16. Stewart, Nora

CLASS HISTORY.

A CLASS without a history would indeed be a very odd class. Finding no one outside the Junior class who was able to write such a history, it becomes the duty of the members of this class to write up ourselves in our own annual. Before many lines of this production have been read, you will find out that we are proud of the fact that we are Juniors. We know that many things are in store for us and how ready we are to battle the difficult things of life.

Well do we remember the time when we entered the Freshman class at the S. I. N. U. Through the corridors, tumbling we went, looking for our class-rooms. The Seniors of that day were to us great people; and so they are to-day. Although we recall many sad experiences while a Freshman, many pleasant ones often come to our minds. But taking it all into consideration we were not so green as we looked to be. We progressed rapidly and soon had *quite a "stand in"* with faculty and friends. By the time we had reached our Sophomore year, great thoughts began to chase each other through our heads. But nothing worthy of mention resulted from these notions, and it was not until we had reached our Junior year that we achieved great fame. Then how quickly we grew!

We began to surprise our teachers by our deep thinking and wonderful answers. We also learned to appreciate long lectures and chapel talks. While the greater part of our time is given to our studies, many pleasant hours are spent in social meetings. The Seniors are too much occupied in commencement dresses and assignment of parts on the program to think of real fun. So it devolves upon the Juniors, who by this time have well learned how to manage their studies so that they need never interfere with a good time and who, being upper classmen, can take privileges that others would never think of taking. Whatever we turn our attention to we generally succeed in having a most hilariously good time.

Our class is composed of sixteen bright, intelligent, good looking members.

CLASS POEM.

I'll chant you a song of the Juniors,
   The grandest class of all,
Of whom you hear many rumors,
   Up there in Normal Hall.

Many a class has had promise,
   Others have dwindled away;
But none are half so famous,
   As this Junior class so gay.

Some reside in distant towns,
   In other parts of the state,
Yet, together we go the rounds,
   Sharing a common fate.

And this is a good thing to do,
   To thus our forces combine,
That we may sooner subdue,
   The [evil] plots of ninety-nine.

The Freshman class, you know,
   Is very great in beauty,
Always waiting to bestow,
   Some gentle act of duty.

When the Freshman comes to school,
   He's just as green as grass;
But a Senior, as a rule,
   He is apt to be too fast.

He thinks the world he holds in fee,
   With all its wealth and knowledge,
Yet, less he knows, it seems to me,
   Than when he entered college.

Now with the Juniors 'tis not so,
   They share one common fate,
And from the first continue to grow,
   Until they finally graduate.

So here's to the Juniors of ninety-nine.
   May their lives bring fame and praise,
And when you manage to have the time,
   Think once of our Normal days.

MUSIC CLASS TRAINING DEPARTMENT.

VIEW LOOKING EAST FROM NORMAL HALL.

YOUNG MEN'S CHRISTIAN ASSOCIATION.

THIS movement originated in London in 1844. Seven years later the first
association in the United States was organized in Boston. The field
has grown until at the present time there are more than five thousand societies distributed over the world, and more than half a million members.

In addition to the general work, there are the College Department,
Railroad Department, work among German young men, and colored young
men.

In 1877 the intercollegiate work was organized; now there are about
525 college associations having a total of 33,000 members.

The Y. M. C. A. of this institution was organized April 25, 1875. For
many years the membership was small and the outlook was discouraging.
The meetings were held in Zetetic Hall until last year when the Board of
Trustees set apart a room for the use of the two associations.

The meetings are held on Wednesdays at noon and the term dues are
25 cents.

It is the aim of the association to make all new students at home and
to look after their spiritual as well as their intellectual welfare.

OFFICERS.

President, John V. Barrow.

Vice-President, Augustus J. Reef.

Corresponding Secretary, Simeon Boomer.

Recording Secretary, Roscoe Baker.

Treasurer, Harry W. Temple.

MEMBERS.

Allen, F. B.
Barnfield, P. S.
Barrow, John V.
Barton, George
Baker, Roscoe
Boggs, V. O.
Boomer, Simeon
Bourland, Thomas
Brainard, Stuart L.
Brandon, Wm. A.
Brinkerhoff, Roland
Brubaker, Loren
Carson, David
Cisne, W. G.
Corzine, Ford
Couch, Maurice
Cowan, J. P.
Cross, K. K.
Davis, James
Demmer, John
Dorsey, C. A.
Ernest, T. R.
Etherton, Jas. M.
Etherton, J. E.
Freeland, H. L.
Gain, O. O.
Gambill, J. M.
Gauter, A. H.
Greathouse, J. W.
Harris, W. O.
Heller, Peter
Higginson, C. M.
Hinderliter, M. L.
House, Oscar
Iles, I. Victor
Kingsbury, H. B.
Kell, Chas.
Karraker, O. M.
Layman, T. J.

Marchildon, John W
Marberry, J. Oscar
Marberry, John L.
Maxwell, T. R.
McConaghie, Thos
McClanahan, Henry F.
McCue, J. Ed.
McKittrick, F. D.
McKnelly, J. I.
Miller, Jno.
Mills, Curtis B.
Moore, Alva
Muckelroy, Renzo
Otey, Jas.
North, Roscoe
Piper, Robert
Pruett, Chas. F.
Rice, A. Z.
Reef, A. J.
Scherer, Geo. E.
Shepherd, A. B.
Sivia, H.
Skaggs, W. W.
Smith, T. B. F.
Stahl, H. F.
Stevenson, Albert
Stevenson, Newton
Stewart, W. E.
Summerville, Ira
Taylor, Charles
Temple, Harry W.
Templeman, Willis
Vaughn, E. B.
Wayman, Kay O.
Webkemeyer, Carl
Whetstone, T. H.
Wilkes, H. C.
Wyatt, R. D.

YOUNG WOMEN'S CHRISTIAN ASSOCIATION.

OFFICERS.

MAY FRYAR, - - - - - President
TILLIE McCONAGHIE, - - - Vice-President
ALICE HAWLEY, - - - - - Secretary
ETHEL CRUSE, - - - - Treasurer

MEMBERS.

Bellamy, Callie
Bonham, Eunice
Bowyer, Hattie
Brewster, Libbie
Brainard, Pearl
Buck, M., Miss
Chandler, Kate
Charlton, Daisy
Coulter, Lena
Cruse, Ethel
Drum, Mrs.
Davis, Pearl
English, Hattie
Etherton, Kate
Ervin, Mary
Fryar, Miss M.
Fryar, May
Foster, Edith
Grove, Bessie
Gant, Anna
Gillespie, Ella
Haldaman, Margaret
Hill, Mabel
Hewitt, Eva

Hill, Nona
Hawthorne, Laura
Hawkins, Lizzie
Hawley, Alice
Jenkins, Ella
Kershaw, Mary
Kelsey, Mary
McConaghie, Tillie
Marvin, Minnie
McLinn, Emma
Mercer, Iva
Palmer, Irene
Pollock, Clara
Pope, Emma
Prather, Sophy
Rust, Mamie
Spence, Bertha
Stone, Blanche
Stewart, Nora
Stewart, Josephine
Salter, Miss Tillie
White, Lottie
Whittenberg, Lulu
Wyatt, Myrtle

Zimmerman, Lily

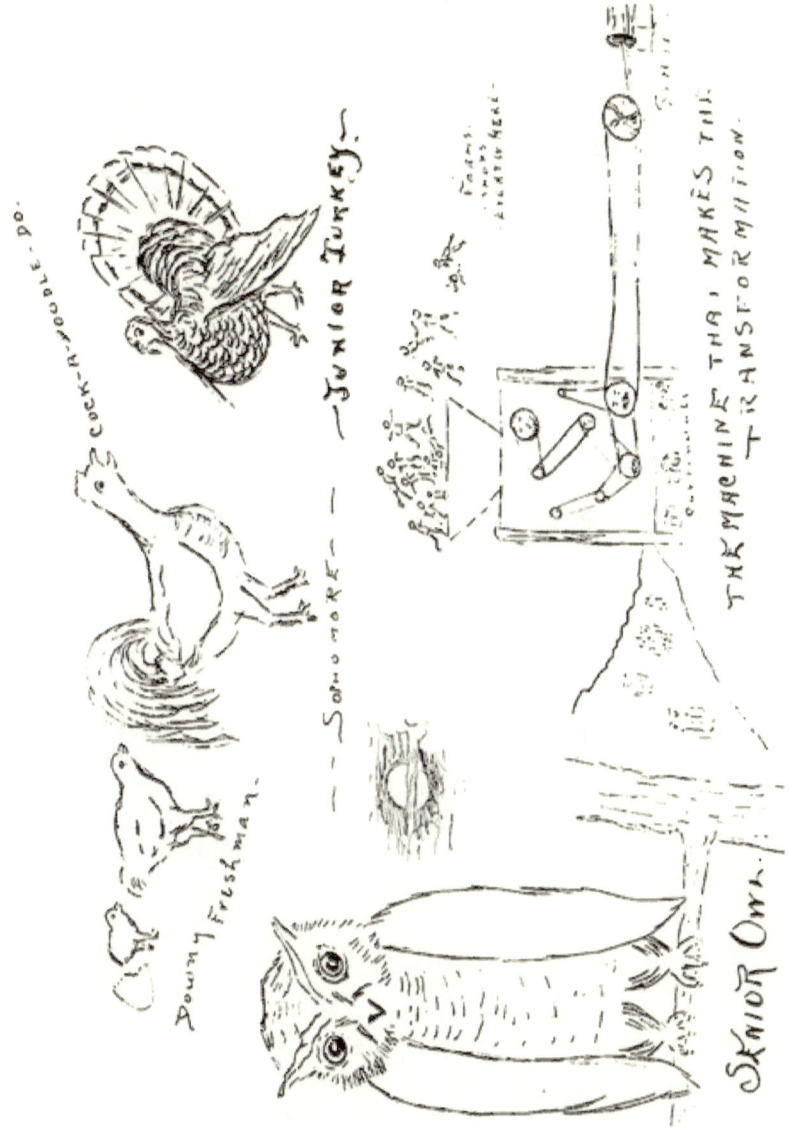

ANNALS 1898-99.

SEPTEMBER.

Sept. 13.— School opens. Y. M. C. A. boys direct giddy freshmen.

Sept. 16.—Societies meet.   Mr. Marberry disagrees with President Etherton of Socratic Society.

Sept. 17.—Reception to new students at Dr. Parkinson's.

Sept. 24.—Y. M. C. A. reception at Prof. Whittington's.

Sept. 28.—Capt. Brush lectures at Chapel on "Battle of San Juan."

OCTOBER.

Oct. 13.—Miss McDonald sings at Chapel.

Oct. 5.—Soldiers from Fourth Illinois visit school.

Oct. 23.—Bulletin Board placed in library.

Oct. 31.—Halloween eve. Faculty serenaded. Janitor patrols campus.

NOVEMBER.

Nov. 5.—Sunshine, rain, clouds, and hail.

Nov. 11.—Judge Wheeler speaks at Chapel on "John Marshall." School council meets.   Dr. De Blois speaks on "The New Profession."

Nov. 15.—The powers decide to allow football.

Nov. 17.—Senior Pruett and Junior Davis redolent with arnica.

Nov. 22.—Cold wave.

Nov. 23.—Students go home to spend Thanksgiving.

Nov. 30.—First snow. Dr. Parkinson cautions the Seniors about snow-balling.

DECEMBER.

Dec. 1.—New song books in Normal Hall.   "Upidee sung".

Dec. 3.—Preparatory foot-ball team defeats Murphysboro High-school team; score, 28 to 0.

Dec. 13.—Capt. Keene lectures in Normal Hall.

Dec. 19.—Members of Geometry class put books under pillows.

Dec. 22.—School closes. No reception. Principal topic, "Did I pass, Mr. Harwood?"

JANUARY.

Jan. 3.—Winter term opens.

Jan. 4.—Classes begin. "The day is cold and dark and dreary; it rains, and the Geometry class is weary."

Jan. 12.—Masonic banquet up town.

Jan. 18.—Y. M. and Y. W. C. A. have luncheon in Art room.

Jan. 24.—Masons attending "School of Instruction," visit Chapel. They ask that students sing "Old Grimes."

Jan. 30.—State Superintendent Freeman lectures at Chapel on "The Teacher and His Work."

FEBRUARY.

Feb. 1.—Western Stars Concert Company at Opera House.

Feb. 9.—Wednesday Club lunches in room 8.

Feb. 10.—President Cook of Normal speaks at Chapel on "The New Profession."

Feb. 13.—Very cold; seventeen below zero. Senior Karraker's ear frozen.

Feb. 19.—Spring weather.

Feb. 22.—Washington's birthday. Dr. Parkinson entertains resident alumni.

MARCH.

March 1.—Measles. A number of students out of school.

March 7.—Bishop Fowler lectures at the Opera House on Abraham Lincoln.

March 11.—Senior class organizes.

March 13.—President Turner of Lincoln University addresses students. Subject, "Brain and Brawn."

March 20.—Dr. Finley speaks at Chapel.

March 21.—Junior class organizes.

March 23.—Winter term closes.

March 28.—Spring term begins.

March 31.—Committee of legislators visits school.

APRIL.

April 3.—Heavy snow. Preps. and Seniors indulge in snow-balling.

April 5.—Seniors adopt class colors.

April 14.—Dr. Willits lectures at Opera House on "Sunshine."

April 20—Tulips on campus in bloom.

April 23.—Arbor day. Address given by President McGee of Cape Girardeau. Normal Seniors plant elm tree on campus. Juniors give yell.

MAY.

May 3.—The Geometry class, composed of Juniors, pronounced the best one (?) ever in University.

May 4.—School dismissed during third hour to see Company C, Fourth Illinois Volunteers, return home. Seniors view train from roof of main building.

May 5.—Southern Illinois High School Oratorical and Athletic Association meets at Carbondale Normal school.

May 6.—School Council of Southern Illinois meets at University.

May 8.—Picture of Senior class taken.

May 10.—Prof. Brownlee's dog, "Porto Rico," runs away. Great excitement at school.

May 12.—Members of Medical Association visit school.

May 13.—JUNIOR ANNUAL goes to press.

OLD LIBRARY.

In Memoriam

FACULTY.

Miss Julia F. Mason, Prin. Prac. School.

Prof. John Bengel, Teacher of German.

Dr. Rob't Allyn, President.

Prof. S. M. Inglis, Math., Rhetoric.

BOARD OF TRUSTEES.

Thos. S. Ridgway, Pres.   Dr. Jas. Roberts, Sec'y.

L. M. Phillips.   Henry Schmidt.

T. O. Johnston.

TREASURER.

John S. Bridges.

PHYSICAL TRAINING CLASS, S. I. N. U.—FIFTH HOUR.

PROF. JOHN HULL.

PROF. JOHN HULL.

PROF. JOHN HULL was the second President of the Southern Illinois State Normal University, succeeding Dr. Allyn in the summer of 1892.

Prof. Hull is a native of Salem, Marion county, Illinois. He had the ordinary advantages of the public schools of a third of a century ago. At the age of about 18 years, he entered the State Normal at Normal with the first entering class. From the Normal he was graduated in due course of time and immediately entered upon the profession of teaching.

He was soon thereafter elected to the superintendency of the schools of McLean county. In this capacity he served a portion of two terms, coming to this school about the second year of its existence. He organized the training department and was connected therewith during his connection with the school. He was especially interested in higher mathematics and usually conducted classes therein, though not required by the course of study.

He also liked to delve in the mysteries of Metaphysics and was for several years in charge of the Pedagogy and Psychology.

When Dr. Allyn resigned in '92, the board selected Prof. Hull as his successor. Prof. Hull had already been selected to have charge of the exhibit of the Southern Illinois Normal at the World's Fair, and the burden of preparing the exhibit now fell upon him. He was ably assisted by the Faculty and the exhibit by this school was universally praised by educators.

At the end of one year's service as president, there was a change in the board and Prof. Hull severed his connection with the school. He was chosen president of the River Falls, Wisconsin, Normal. Here he served one year when, by reason of ill health, he resigned and went into the Rocky Mountains. Later he located in New Whatcom, on Puget Sound, Washington, where he is now engaged as editor of a daily paper.

Dr. H. A. Everest.

HARVEY W. EVEREST, A.M., LL.D.

HARVEY W. EVEREST, A.M., LL.D., was the third President of the Southern Illinois State Normal University.

Dr. Everest was a native New Yorker, but early moved into Ohio. During the stormy days preceding the sixties he was a student of Bethany College, Virginia. His anti-slavery sentiments were too strong to suit the college management, and he and nine other students withdrew from the school. Dr. Everest afterwards finished his course in Oberlin College. He had, meanwhile, done considerable teaching. On finishing his course in Oberlin he went into Hiram Collage and was associated with Garfield. Garfield entered the army and Dr. Everest took his place as president. In this capacity he served for several years. In succeeding years he served as President of Butler University, Kentucky University, Eureka College, and Garfield University.

When Prof. Hull severed his connection with this school, Dr. Everest was chosen as president, which position he held for four years.

Dr. Everest was a man of broad culture and of extensive practical knowledge. He was a deep thinker and has incorporated his thoughts in several volumes, among which his "Divine Demonstration" is the best known. He was also an orator of no ordinary powers. His power as an orator seemed to lie in his ability to deal tenderly with the common experiences of the race and to discover and lay bare the philosophy of human duty.

The school prospered under Dr. Everest's management, and had it not been for declining health he would probably yet have been directing the interests of the school.

On his retirement in the summer of '97 he took the chair of Bible study in Drake University where he yet remains. Word comes that his health is still poor. He left in Egypt a host of ardent admirers who will always be glad to hear of his success.

FRESHMAN-SOPHOMORE CLASS.

Colors: Pink and Gold. Motto: Unknown.

Class Yell: "Shorthorse Seniors,
Bighead Juniors,
Blowhards all of you,
We are none of you."

President, - - - - John V. Barrow.
Vice-President, - - - Belle Smith.
Secretary, - - - - Chesley Boggs.
Treasurer, - - - Lillian Teeter.

LIST OF MEMBERS.

Allen, H. John
Asher, Grace L.
Barrow, John V.
Bellamy, John
Boggs, Vivian
Boggs, Chesley,
Bowyer, Emma
Brinkerhoff, Roland
Brubaker, Loren
Calhoon, Nora
Campbell, Jas. S.
Casper, Geo. F.
Cook, Evelyn
Cook, Lillian B.
Cook, Nettie
Cross, Daisy
Davis, Pearl
Denton, Laurence
Dillinger, Carrie
Etherton, Harmon
Etherton, Julia W.
Frazier, Lucy
Gaston, W. T.
Gurley, M. A.
Hill, Stanley
Hopper, Olive
Houts, Mabel
Johnson, Laura
Kanada, Ella
Lightfoot, Ella
Lightfoot, Anna
Mackey, J. Frank

Miller, Effie M
Nelson, Anna C.
Nelson, Marion
Norfleet, B. Frank
Otey, Chas. R.
Perce, Amelia A.
Perce, Clara
Phillips, Grace
Roberts, Flora
Robertson, Essie
Roach, Frank L.
Raynor, May
Robinson, Chas.
Skaggs, W. W.
Slater, Lucile B.
Smith, Ada I.
Smithe, I. Belle
Smith, Beulah
Sprague, Jessie
Summerville, Ira
Teeter, Lillian
Thomas, J. Ed.
Thornton, Nellie
Vaugh, E. Bebb
Walker, Chas. A.
Walther, J. A. B.
Whetstone, J. H.
Whittenberg, Lulu
Willms, T. B.
Wyatt, Myrtle
White, Lotta
Zimmerman, Lily

OLD ART ROOM.

THE OBSCURE HERO.

When the battleship, the Bancroft,
  Was pounding down old San Juan,
Something crooked as it does oft
  Got into her boilers then.

As the Bancroft, strong, withdrew
  From the murky smoke and fight,
Up came the little Castine, true;
  Her guns belched flames of light.

But down below, a little seam,
  Made by a loose boiler tap,
Let on the fire the hissing steam—
  An explosion sure will hap.

Men stood around with faces pale;
  "Bank the fires! Turn off forced-draft."
'Tis Huntley, a boilermaker, hale,
  The people thought him daft.

"Bank the fires! Turn off forced-draft!"
  With that, he caught a plank
And threw it into the furnace door,
  Across the raging mass.

On this, into that hell he crawled;
  Three minutes worked he there;
Then half came out and half was hauled,
  With burning flesh and singed hair.

The leak was stopped—The draft turned on,
  The ship sped on into the fight;
The captain knew not what was done,
  Nor felt but all was right.

He did his duty. He was not dead;
  But a true hero was he;
"One life for many," as he said—
  'Twas offered tho' not given.

NOTE.- No other name is known than boilermaker Huntley of Norfolk, Va.

PHYSICAL TRAINING CLASS, S. I. N. U.—SEVENTH HOUR.

ZETETIC HALL.

ZETETIC LITERARY SOCIETY.

ON Sept. 19, 1874, ten young men and four young women met, framed the constitution and by-laws, and elected the first officers of the Zetetic Society. Those who have the honor of being charter members are Messrs. John Dean, John Wood, John E. Iles, J. N. Brown, Flannigan, Roberts, Thompson, McAually, Kane, Abernathy, and Misses Morrow, Roberts, Sherman and Wright.

By the light of two tallow candles the first regular meeting was held in a recitation room of the old building. Early in the same term the Board of Trustees set apart a room for its use.

In spite of these small beginnings the society grew and prospered, and only after a quarter of a century has passed away do we begin to realize how well the foundation of our beloved society was laid. It depends on personal efforts what the character will be, and every idea of the Zetetic Society is to develop the powers of the intellect and educate the head and heart together, so that each character may be rounded and full and that every one who goes forth from its hall may be an honor to his society and a blessing to his country.

The old members are scattered throughout the Union, and everywhere they occupy positions of honor and trust. The present members are active and earnest and never fail to entertain the visitors who throng its hall.

Its well furnished and beautiful hall, its glorious past, successful present and bright future, prove that all things come to those who * "LEARN TO LABOR AND TO WAIT."

---

* Motto.

THE SPHINX.

ZETETIC LITERARY SOCIETY.

OFFICERS.

President, I. Victor Iles.

Vice-President, E. G. Ferrill.

Recording Secretary, A. H. Burton.

Corresponding Secretary, Winifred Schmalhausen.

Editor, Harry W. Temple.

Treasurer, John Demmer.

Critic, J. I. McKnelly.

Librarian, Gregg Garrison.

Usher, John W. Marchildon.

Chorister, Emma McLin.

Chaplain, H. L. Freeland.

MEMBERS.

Baker, Roscoe	Dixon, Stella	Iles, I. Victor	Reef, Augustus J.
Birkholz, Chas.	Draper, N. W.	Jenkins, Zenas	Rice, A. Z.
Black, Fanny	Duis, Mary	Johnson, Bessie	Robinson, Chas.
Black, J. T.	Etherton, Harmon	Johnson, Samuel	Scherer, Geo. E.
Blevins, R. A.	Ernest, T. R.	Keesee, Leota	Schmalhausen, Winif'd
Bourland, Thos.	Ferrill, E. G.	Kell, C. S.	Slater, Lucile
Bowyer, Hattie	Freeland, H. L.	Kershaw, Mary	Sprague, Jessie
Brandon, Wm. A.	Fryar, May	Kingsbury, H. B.	Stone, C. Blanche
Brewster, Libbie M.	Garrison, Erma	Kirk, Mamie	Storment, L. G.
Brown, L. W.	Garrison, Grace	Launer, June	Swofford, John C.
Brown, Robt. E.	Garrison, Gregg	Launer, Stella	Tanner, Lillian
Burton, A. H.	Greathouse, J. W.	Marchildon, John W.	Teeter, Lillian
Carmichael, Alice	Grove, Bessie L.	Marron, Minnie	Temple, Harry W.
Chandler, Kate	Harris, W. O.	McKinney, Henry	Templeman, Willis
Cisne, W. G.	Hiller, J. A.	McKittrick, F. D.	Thompson, Elizabeth
Cook, Evelyn	Hill, Mabel	McKnelly, J. I.	Thompson, Fred
Cook, Nettie	Hill, Stanley	McLin, Emma	Thompson, Lavera
Crow, Waller	Hobbs, Thos.	Mertz, Bertie	Toler, Samuel
Davis, Clara	Hooker, Mrs.	Miller, Effie	Williams, Maude
Davis, Pearl	Hooker, Zetta	Montgomery, J. T.	Willms, T. B.
Davis, Roy F. B.	Hopper, Olive	Moore, Alva	Wray, Jerome
Demmer, John	House, Oscar	Palmer, Irene	

New Museum.

SOCRATIC HALL.

THE SOCRATIC LITERARY SOCIETY.

THE Socratic Society has reached its twenty-fourth anniversary. Through all the years it has increased in numbers until at present it has a large membership. The record during the past year is an honor to every one who bears the name of Socratic, and a source of gratification to its many friends.

The members have pursued their work with an energy which means success, and as a result the society has advanced beyond its friends' highest hopes. Each one has striven for individual advancement, not forgetting the interest of the society as a unit. During the entire year the members have worked together harmoniously, thus showing their interest in one another's welfare.

The programs have consisted of the lines of work mentioned in the preamble of the constitution; viz: recitations, essays, music, debates, orations and extemporaneous addresses. The different members seem to have chosen different phases as their special line of work, and have given almost their entire attention to that work. The essays, debates and orations have shown thought and careful study. The recitations and music have been a pleasing feature.

The programs have been made more attractive, and their strength has been greatly increased by the aid which the members of the faculty and some of the alumni have so cheerfully given.

Much good has been accomplished during the past year, and the prospects for the future are bright.

THE SOCRATIC LITERARY SOCIETY.

The following are the officers and members now in attendance at the Normal.

OFFICERS.

Edward L. Blake, President.

T. B. F. Smith, Vice-President.

Myrtle Wyatt, Recording Secretary.

Simeon Boomer, Corresponding Secretary.

Renzo Muckleroy, Critic.

Lulu Whittenberg, Chaplain.

Mabel Houts, Pianist.

J. Frank Mackey, Usher.

MEMBERS.

Frank Allen.
M. R. Batman.
Eugene Barrow.
John V. Barrow.
John Bellamy.
Welcome Bonham.
Archie Bonham.
Vivian O. Boggs.
C. A. Boggs.
Stuart Brainard.
Pearl Brainard.
Loun Brubaker.
Roland Brinkerhoff.
Simeon Boomer.
Helen Boomer.
Kate Beecher.
C. L. Blake.
Ethel Cruse.
Harry E. Campbell.
James Campbell.
Lena Coulter.
K. K. Cross.
Daisy Cross.
D. H. Carson.
H. S. Davis.

Guy Dillo.
Carrie Dillinger.
Mary Davis.
Lizzie Elder.
James Etherton.
Hattie English.
Edith Foster.
J. M. Gambill.
Roy Gregg.
Ella Gillespie.
Annie Gant.
M. A. Gurly.
Duff Hartwell.
Margaret Haldaman.
Jennie Hill.
Alice Hawly.
Margaret Holden.
Mabel Houts.
Agnes Hinkley.
Cora Hart.
Mary Hawkins.
M. L. Hinderliter.
Ada Higgins.
Madge Higgins.
D. C. Jones.

Laura Johnson.
Mary Kelsey.
Davis Kell.
Ida Kell.
Orville Karraker.
Annie Lightfoot.
Thomas J. Layman.
Iva Mercer.
Minnie Marvin.
T. R. Maxwell.
Thomas McConghie.
Tillie McConghie.
John Miller.
Renzo Muckleroy.
J. Oscar Marberry.
Gordon Murphey.
Maggie Miller.
J. Frank Mackey.
Claude Norris.
Annie Nelson.
F. Norfleet.
J. R. Phillips.
Charles Pruett.
May Putnam.
Annie A. Perce.

Stella Roach.
F. L. Roach.
Edith Roe
Flora Roberts.
Essie Robertson.
Kate Spam.
John Yost Stotlar.
Nora Stewart.
Josephine Stewart.
Bertha Spence.
T. B. F. Smith.
W. W. Skaggs.
Gasper Stocton.
H F. Stahl.
Arthur Taylor.
J. Ed. Thomas.
Nellie Thorton.
E. B. Vaughan.
J. A. B. Walther.
Lulu Whittenberg.
O. M. Wells.
Gilbert Wise.
C. W. Webkemeyer.
Myrtle Wyatt.
Lizzie Zimmerman.

OLD HISTORY ROOM.

OUR FACULTY.

Dr. Parkinson is president of this institution,
The best and the wisest in all this wide nation;
He gives us advice and holds us to duty,
And the result of his rule is diligence in study.

Professor Shryock is an ideal man,
Find another such a teacher if you can;
A frown for a failure, a smile for success,
Of all your good teachers, we know he's the
    best.

Professor Smith is a favorite with all,
A teacher and friend of the great and the
    small;
To him for sympathy the poor student goes,
Kind words and encouragement professor
    bestows.

Professor Davis has wit at command,
To apply to all students and teachers on hand;
He is always smiling, good natured and kind,
A teacher just suited to most student's mind.

And we'll give you leave to look the world
    over,
A teacher like Brownlee you'll never discover,
For elocution and music we know he's the
    one,
And he's the best reading teacher under the
    sun.

Professor Harwood is a favorite with some,
Who regard mathematics a pleasure and fun,
Yet some there are whose knowledge is poor,
But receive from Professor the best help I
    am sure.

Professor Kirk rules his students with looks,
But for him you're compelled to pursue your
    books;
Though he is kind and the student's best
    friend,
You must know your lessons from beginning
    to end.

And there's Professor Colyer, so earnest and
    good,
A teacher we like, as every one should;
He has no favorites, as some teachers do,
But to every student is honest and true.

Some like Professor Allen the best of all,
For Latin and German upon him they call;
We know there's no other teacher equal to him,
Unless it's our teacher who governs the Gym.

Professor Whittington is jolly and glad,
No student with him ever tries to look sad;
For in the Gymnasium far vanishes our sorrow,
It's joy for to-day, with no thought of the morrow.

And there's Professor French, so good and kind,
Who—nowhere else in this state you could find,
A teacher of 'ologies with so much patience,
To govern the student by such a soft cadence.

And there is another, the youngest and best,
We would not give him up if you took all the
    rest;
He knows mathematics without a doubt,
It's Professor Alvis we speak about.

And now the lady teachers, all in rhyme,
I'll tell you of, if I find ample time;
For last is best, you know 'tis said,
So lend your attention till my rhyme you have
    read,

Miss Buck on the subject of grammar is wise,
A teacher like her every student should prize;
Asleep or awake she can grammar teach,
And she always frowns at awkward speech.

Miss Fryar, the librarian, is pleasant and sweet,
And an hour spent with her we regard as a treat;
Where a topic may be found she always can tell,
For she knows every book and paper full well.

Miss McNeil knows music by heart,
And well she knows how to teach this art;
She is quiet, good-natured, mild and pleasant,
And music we have when she is present.

Miss Wertz and Miss Parks the children keep,
And 'tis seldom a child is made to weep;
For each of these teachers is pleasant and
    merry,
And by them this room is made bright and
    cheery.

In the northwest corner, on the second floor,
Is Miss Salter, a teacher whom we all adore;
For she with a smile every student does greet,
Without her our faculty would be incomplete

GIRLS' BASKET BALL TEAMS, S. I. N. U.

UNIVERSITY GLEE CLUB.

CISNE.   BARTON.   MUCKLEROY.   LEE. J.   BOOHER.   SMITH. J.   BELL.   MABERRY.
LEE.   ALVIS. J.   FRELLAND.   TEMPLE.   STUWART.   PROF. SMITH (Director).

THE NORMAL GLEE CLUB.

FIRST TENORS.

Harry J. Alvis,
W. Alonzo Etherton,
H. L. Freeland,
Ardell Lee.

FIRST BASS.

Walter E. Stewart,
J. Frank Mackey,
Geo. W. Smith,
Harry W. Temple.

SECOND TENORS.

Arthur Lee,
Willis G. Cisne,
A. H. Burton,
W. Gordon Murphey.

SECOND BASS.

Thos. B. F. Smith,
J. Oscar Marberry,
A. Z. Rice,
Simeon Boomer.

The club was organized in the Spring of '98. The membership this year is very nearly the same as that of last year. The club has given several public recitals and it has been received with enthusiasm by the music loving people. The club sings first-class music, and has given an impetus to male quartette singing throughout Egypt. The credit for this success is due to the director, Prof. Geo. W. Smith, who is very popular among the boys.

THE FACULTY QUARTETTE.

MISS M. NEIL.   PROF. ALVIS.   MISS WERTZ.   PROF. SMITH.

MUSICAL.

FACULTY QUARTETTE.

Soprano—Miss McNeil.   Alto—Miss Wertz.

Tenor—H. J. Alvis.   Bass—Geo. W. Smith.

ZETETIC QUARTETTE.

First Tenor—H. L. Freeland.   First Bass—Harry Temple.

Second Tenor—W. G. Cisne.   Second Bass—A. Z. Rice.

SOCRATIC QUARTETTE.

Soprano—Tillie McConaghie.   Tenor—H. F. Stahl.

Alto—Nora Stewart.   Bass—J. Oscar Marberry.

UNIVERSITY OCTETTE.

Director—Prof. James H. Brownlee.

Sopranos—Bessie Johnson, Hattie Bowyer.

Altos—Mabel Houts. Emma McLin.

Tenors—Robert Brownlee, W. Alonzo Etherton.

Bassos—A. Z. Rice, Simeon Boomer.

THE SENIORS PLANT A TREE.

The Seniors had a hedge row,
And it grew, and it grew,
And it grew on Thompson's farm,
And the hedge row did no harm.

In the hedge row was an elm,
And *it* grew, and it grew ;
And it had a grape vine 'round it,
'Till the Seniors came and found it.

'Twas on Arbor Day they took it,
Oh how sad, oh how sad ;
When they took it from its mate,
To the campus by the gate.

When hot weather comes again,
It will wilt, it will wilt ;
The Seniors then will gather 'round it,
And they'll wish they hadn't found it.

Now ye Seniors when you go
From our midst to other schools,
And help on Arbor Day you need,
Send for Junior turnip seed.

Junior Turnip.

SENIOR TREE

DRAMA.

THE UNIVERSITY OF HADES.

Translated from the Original Greek of Aristophanes.

BY GUSTAVUS ADOLPHUS ALGEBRAICUS

——————(Translator's preface omitted by request of the Chancellor.)——————

DRAMMATIS PERSONÆ.

Xenophon. - - - President University.	H. W. S., - - Supt. Public Schools connected with University.
Pythagoras, . - - - Mathematics.	
Euclid, - - - - Assistant.	F. H. C., - - - - Assistant.
Euler, - - - - - Assistant.	Shakespoke, - - An old playwright.
A. P. W., - - Professor of Music.	Tennyson. - - Poet-Laureate to Pluto.
J. K., - - - Physical Torture.	Cicero, - - - State's Attorney.
D. B. P., - Assistant, specialty, golf.	Cæsar, - - - Retired Soldier.
S. B. W., - Philosophy and Pedagogy.	Henry VIII, - - Only Mormon above Tartarus.
Hegel, - - - - - Assistant.	
Herbert. - - - Assistant.	C. E. A , - - - A new arrival.
G. H. F., - - - - Star-gazer.	S. E. H., - - - A new arrival.
G. W. S., - Principal Girls' Academy.	Place, - - - - - Hades.

Time   Any time the next 500 years.

ACT. I.

SCENE 1.

Pythagoras. Euclid. Euler.

PYTHAGORAS.

Hello ! Who is this little man that walks
So briskly on thro' these Elysian fields ?
He seems to have a sober look as those
Who search for truth. He knows, I'll bet
   the proof
For this: The sum of the squares on the legs
   of a right
Triangle is equal to the squares on the hy-
   pothenuse.
He must know that, for I it was who found it

EUCLID.

O, he is one of those barbarians:
He wears such heavy beard. I know he
   knows
Not me. For my acquaintance is not made
By such. 'Tis downy youths who me do most
   delight.

EULER.

I wonder if he ever heard of me.

Enter S. E. H.

S. E. H.

Of all this company none is more
Admired by pupils of geometry
Than he, who, blind, could see what still to
   them
Is dark. But still, I think, he found the
   truth

Who said, though his name is Etherton,that
   you,
Herr Euler, saw because you were thus
   blind.

PYTHAGORAS.

Good sir, I speak with Greek and Latin
   modesty.
Why should you rank this Swiss man above
   me ?
Me ! who in dark and light did show to all
Who would believe that our small globe is
   round,
And less than sun and stars, though some
   do that
Deny. They know me not at all. Am not
I then far greater than this Swiss ? Say that.

S. E. H.

Well, yes, and no. Yes, because you were a
   broader
Student. No, because you were not blind.

EUCLID.

O, new immortal, you indeed are wise,
For you have kept the favor of them both.
Pray, did you not perpetuate my name
Among those students of geometry ?

S. E. H.

O, yes. Your pictured bust did hang above
My desk ; and every day or other day
I spake to them of you as one who in
The world's great galaxy of characters
Did stand among the noblest.

ACT. I.—CONTINUED.

Enter Messenger.

MESSENGER.

My lord Pythagoras, your class doth wait
Your coming, great and mighty professor.

PYTHAGORAS.

This class of mine, O, worthy Professor Har-
wood—
For such indeed you are I know by verses
From one Thomas Layman, who wrote
An arc of poetry—

It did please Satan to create
A room to be known as number 8.
That when people got hot in after ages,
It might be cool to the Normal sages.

But sir, this class is a class of beautiful
girls;
And though I never was married on earth,
I soon, methinks, shall take to wife a fair
And beautiful lass named Irene.
She knows geometry fairly well, and I gave
Her a grade because, you know, she was so
beautiful.

[*Exit with messenger.*

Curtain.

SCENE II.

*Same scene. H. W. S., G. W. S., F. H. C.,
Shakespoke, Tennyson, Julius Cæsar.*

G. W. S.

Good sirs, I have a moment off from my
Most arduous duties. Girls indeed are trou-
blesome.

F. H. C.

And yet, my lord, you are best fitted for
The place. Sir Julius, thou mighty man
To whom all men do turn, who liv'st in his-
tory
The peer of any great bad man, pray tell
Me, did you kill friend Cicero?

CÆSAR.

No, sir;
There comes the noble orator with Henry,
sir.

Enter Cicero and Henry VIII.

G. W. S.

O, king, there is a thing I long have longed
To ask you for. Pray tell how you do man-
age
With your wives down here?

HENRY VIII.

I live with one, one day,
And with the next the next. And then on
Sunday
I have just one day left. To-day my time
Is given to that Dutch girl. You see I'm
out.

To-morrow do I go to live with Anne
Of Cleves. That day I'll stay at home.

H. W. S.—(*Aside to Tennyson.*)

O, great,
O, noble man, whom I do most delight
To read, does not this make you awfully
Tired?

TENNYSON—(*Aside to H. W. S.*)

Ah, well, good sir, I have my Princess now;
And I can much endure if I can find
My love at home.

CÆSAR.

Friend Colyer, let good Cicero confess
If I did do him wrong.

CICERO.

No, no, good sir;
Great Cæsar was a gentleman. And no
True gentleman can do the least that might
Offend the state. But stay, who comes ad-
vancing
Thro' the mist that overhangs the river Styx?
By his fair locks he is an Englishman.
By his great nose he knows what Latin
means.

Enter C. E. A.

C. E. A.

Yea, good Cicero—for by your toga
And your attitude I know that thou art he—
I oft have taught the boys to prize you as
An orator.

CÆSAR.

Yea, but, good sir, and did you teach the
boys
That Shakespoke did perpetrate a most
Offensive lie? It is a thing I ne'er
Have gotten o'er.

C. E. A.

Yes, yes, O, Julius; and had
A boy who read your commentaries through
And said that they were better than was
Dickens.
—And Georgie Washington Professor Smith,
What do you in this climate warm?

G. W. S.

I am,
Good Carl, the president of a girl's academy.

F. H. C.

And most fit, sir, for the place.

C. E. A.

And you, sir, what are you?

F. H. C.

I, sir, assist in taking care of children
Below the seventh grade.

C. E. A.

And who above?

ACT I.—Continued.

F. H. C.

Professor Schryock does preside in teaching
The young idea how to shoot.

G. W. S.

We will
Have a meeting of the faculty to-night,
And you may meet the heads of this great
University.

F. H. C.

Miss Wertz has in the college course
The chair of music.

H. W. S.

Come, let us hie unto the club that Bangs
On earth did write about.

(*Exit omnes*)

ACT II.

SCENE I. *President's office in the University of Hades.*

Xenophon, Euclid, Euler, J. K., who has just won the 100 yard dash from Achilles, G. W. S., A. P. W., S. B. W., Herbart, Hegel, D. B. P., G. H. F., and others of the faculty of the University of Hades.

Enter H. W. S. and C. E. A., Pythagoras and S. E. H.

XENOPHON.

The house will come to order.

PYTHAGORAS.

Ladies and gentlemen, I have the honor
Of placing before your august majesty
A man from earth who us can tell how goes
It up above. He is a man who once
Did teach the young idea how to shoot.
He taught indeed arithmetic and bless'd
Old algebra. Geometry he did beat in,
Into their empty heads. His name is Harwood.

XENOPHON.

Stand forth, Professor Harwood. Gentlemen,
Some of this goodly company do know the
man already.
When business cares are done you may with
him
Converse. But in mine absence, so I hear,
It was on Arbor Day, it seems that some
Did so object unto the Juniors' fun
That my good vice, old Doctor Arnold of
Rugby,
Did feel compelled to ask those men to stop
Their demonstrations 'fore they had been
begun.

Now will you please explain your course,
those who
Did thus object?

—. —.

I, sir, can easily explain my course:
A senior grave, his name was John, came to
Me sobbing piteously, a thing not well
Befit to senior dignity. And when
I did inquire the cause, he was afraid
The Junior boys would mock his chum that
afternoon.
I have been in a university on earth,
And there, sir, this same thing did happen;
And then, as now, I did object, for such
Things are unseemly, sir. No, sir, not I,
On earth or in Hades, can find a thing,
A single thing, that e'er will justify
A Junior class in living—or having its picture taken.
They are to me as an abomination.
And even then the young jay-hawkers,
The crazy gumps, did yell, and so dispell
The finest thoughts that e'er did come into
My mind; that came from that senior's oration.

G. W. S.

And I, sir, Xenophon, was one that did
Encourage Juniors, for 'tis best to have class
spirit.

XENOPHON.

—. —., consider that you have been sat
Upon. Now let that matter drop. And now
You may converse.

[*Reception style. Shake hands, talk, laugh, say you have a good time, turn around and do it all over again.*]

Curtain.

FINIS.

PROF. ALVIS. BRINKERHOFF. DAVIS. CAPT. PRIETT. RHES. HARTWELL. PROF. WHITTINGTON.
COACH. R. H. J. B. MANAGER.

FREELAND. MEDLIN. CRAWSHAW. HUNSAKER. WALKER. CLIFTON. STEELE.
R. E. R. T. R. G. CENTER. L. G. L. T. L. E.

FOOT-BALL, 1898.

Full Back,	-	-	-		-	F. C. Pruett, Captain
Right Half,	-	-	-	-	-	Roland Brinkerhoff
Left Half,	-	-	-	-	-	Hosea Boles
Quarter,	-	-	-	-	-	Roy F. B. Davis
Right End,	-	-	-	-	-	H. L. Freeland
Right Tackle,	-	-	-	-	-	- Medlin
Right Guard,	-	-	-	-	-	Dean Crawshaw
Center,	-	-	-	-	-	- Hunsaker
Left Guard,	-	-	-	-	-	Oscar Walker
Left Tackle,	-	-	-	-	-	Otis Clifton
Left End,	-	-	-	-	-.	Howard Steele

Brinkerhoff got his eye peeled, and in order to go to sleep propped up the lower lid with toothpicks.

THE SUBSTITUTE'S RUN.

THEY lined up at the end of the second half. No point had yet been made. The substitute was left half-back. The ball was Carbondale's. Then the captain sang out those magic numbers, 4, 99, 44, 30. A push, a tangle, a flying mass of heels and arms and heads, and around the end shot the substitute half. There was one minute left, and ninety yards between him and the goal. A man flew out of the struggling mass to stop him ; with a little sprint the substitute shot past him and sped on down the field and fell exhausted between the posts. The touchdown was made, the time was up, the victory won. The substitute was Boles.

After the game.

COMMENCEMENT WEEK.

The twenty-fifth anniversary of the S. I. S. N. U., is to be a glorious week. The program is as follows:

ORDER OF EXERCISES.

JUNE 11th.—Sunday Forenoon: Baccalaureate Sermon, Dr. Richard Edwards. Sunday Evening: Address before the Christian Associations.

JUNE 12th.—Monday Forenoon: Exhibitons of the Physical Training Department, and the Grammar Grades of the Practice School. Monday Afternoon: Lower grades of the Practice School, and Physical Training Department. Monday Evening: Exhibition of Zetetic Society.

JUNE 13th.—Tuesday Forenoon: Class Day Exercises and Junior Yells. Tuesday Afternoon: Non-graduate Exercises. Tuesday Evening: Exhibition of Socratic Society.

JUNE 14th.—Wednesday Forenoon: Reunion of the twenty-four graduating Classes. Wednesday Afternoon: Alumni Business Meeting, and Alumni Banquet. Wednesday Evening: Alumni Public Addresses.

JUNE 15th.—Thursday Forenoon: Commencement Oration, Dr. White; Presentation of Diplomas, Jos. P. Wheeler. Thursday Evening: Opening meeting of Southern Illinois Teachers' Association.

Before Examination   During Ex.   After Ex. grade=90   After Ex. 65.

UNIVERSITY CALENDAR.

1899.

June 19. — Summer term begins.   Sept. 12. —Fall term opens.
July 28. - Summer term ends.   Dec. 21. —Christmas vacation begins·

1900.

Jan. 2.—Winter term opens.   June 13.—Alumni Reunion.
March 22. - Spring vacation.   June 14.—Twenty-sixth Annual Com-
March 27.—Spring term opens.   mencement of the S. I.
June 10.—Baccalaureate Sunday.   N. U. with commence-
June 11.—Socratic Entertainment.   ment oration.
June 12.—Zetetic Entertainment.

A Club chicken.

Using Club Biscuit

The Board.

FARE-YE-WELL.

Have you laughed enough? If not, laugh now. We feel very funny. If you want to know how we look when we are tired, see opposite page. Many things have conduced to making this a brilliant book, mainly such things as "Now look here fellows, this must be —— etc." "Oh bosh," "Rats," "Well I don't want to discourage you, but we must be conservative," "I won't put in that picture," and such like.

Our thanks are due to the editors of the Annuals of Carleton College at Northfield, Minn., of "Knox Gale '98" for the various ideas, though we have never copied. Our thanks are also very heartily tendered to Professors Allen and Smith for their energetic and intelligent assistance in arrangement and management. SO LONG.

www.ingramcontent.com/pod-product-compliance
Lightning Source LLC
Chambersburg PA
CBHW020028030726
47499CB00007B/2329